NOT Enough For QUEEN FLUff

by **Rachel Lyon**

illustrated by **Catalina Echeverri**

For Daisy, Grace & George,
(a.k.a. 'the Lyon cubs')
with oodles of love R.L.

For Will,
with all my love
C.E.

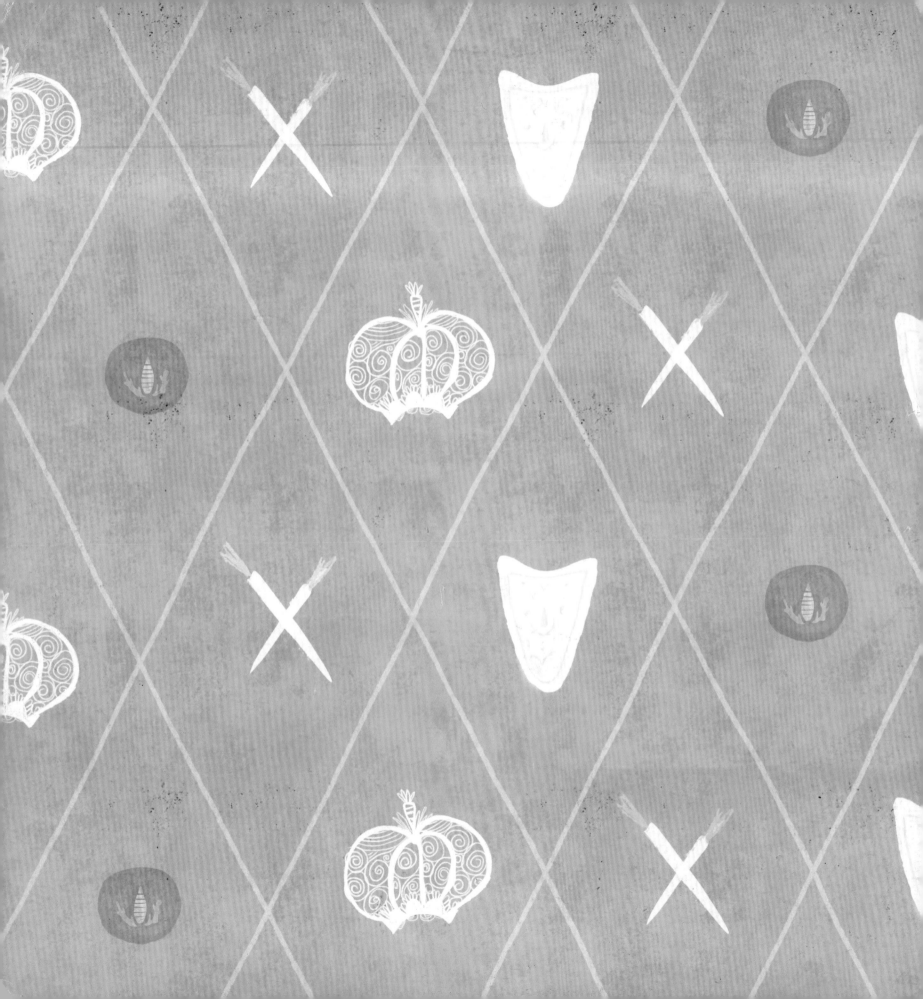

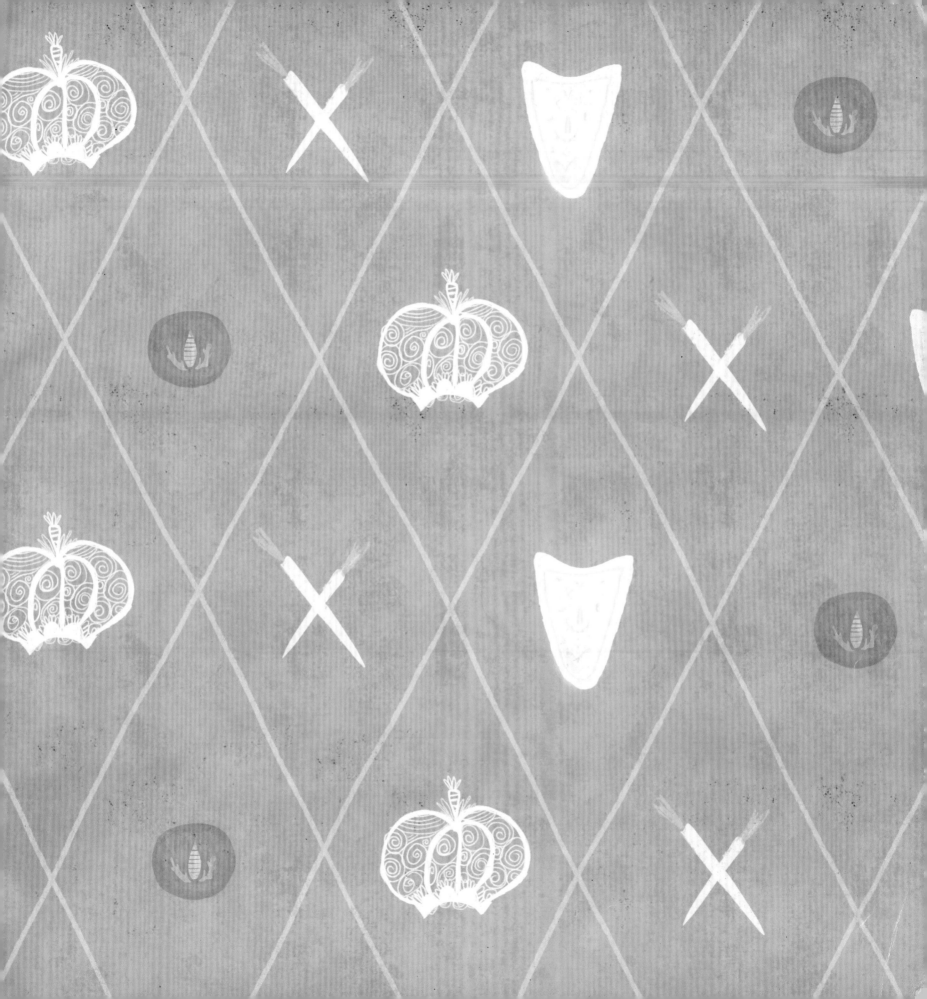

Queen Fluff was the fanciest bunny in town.

She had servants, a stagecoach and quite a big crown.

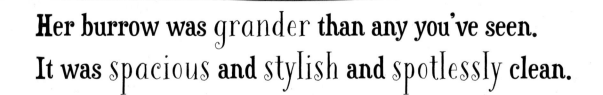

Her burrow was grander than any you've seen.
It was spacious and stylish and spotlessly clean.

She had all the comforts a Queen could afford,
but this Queen was lonely and this Queen was bored.

She longed for a journey, a trip somewhere new
so she sent out a note to each bunny she knew:

I want somewhere fancy to lay my fine head.

A fabulous burrow, a four-poster bed,

and three times a day I require a feast,

an a-la-carte menu, ten-courses, at least!

I'll visit each burrow, perfection I'll seek,

I'll pick out my favourite and stay for a week.

My servants are ready, my bags will be packed,

so bunnies, get busy and clean up your act!

Queen Fluff

BUNNYSHIRE

But out in the Kingdom, the bunnies were poor,
they sat on their bottoms and slept on the floor.
They could not afford to play host to a Queen
who liked everything

fancy and lavish and clean.

So, rather than rushing around to impress,
they tried to deter her by making more mess
and all through the Kingdom they ran to and fro,
taking **thistles** and **nettles**
(and **worse!**) down below.

The Queen, in her spotless, royal burrow, meanwhile, was packing her bags, with a skip and a smile.

The Royal Burrow

The stagecoach was ready, the swans were in place,

so she climbed in with pleasure and set off at pace.

Bunnyshire

The bunnies were waiting, and gave a slight wink,

for they knew what they'd done and they knew what she'd think.

"I'm here," she said, proudly, "I've come to inspect,

and see which fine burrow I'd like to select."

She came to the first hole,
jumped down in a dash...

Only to scamper straight out in a flash.
"It's dreadful!" she bellowed,
"I'm not staying there!"

"I was stung on the bottom
while trying the chair!"

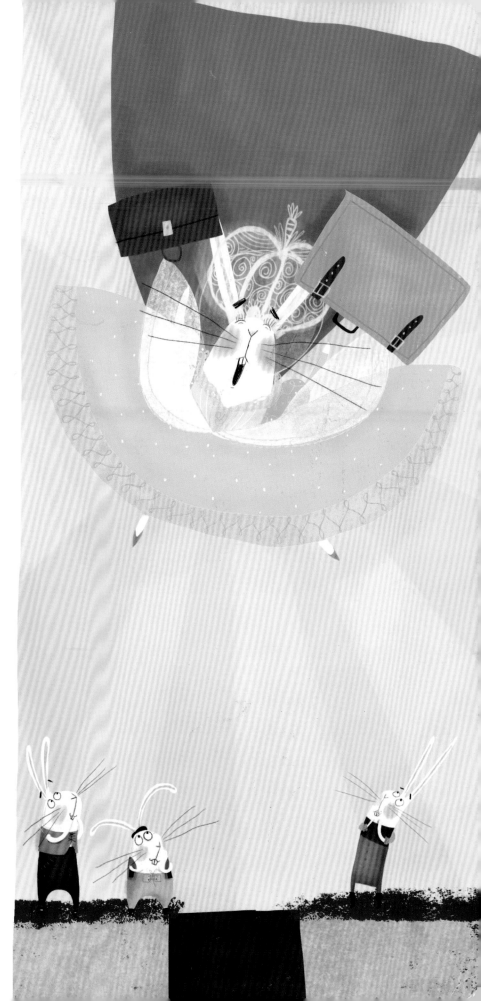

"The fanciest burrow?
Not likely, no way!

Queen Fluff is not coming to
your place to stay!"

She ran down the next hole with eager delight
but hurried straight out with a look of sheer **fright**.
"It's awful," she shouted, "more so than the first!
I cannot believe it, it's really the **worst**!"

"There were **toads** on the table and **fleas** at my feet
and for dinner they offered me bug broth to eat!"

"The fanciest burrow? Not nearly, no way!
Queen Fluff is not coming to your place to stay!"

"If the next hole's no better, I'm leaving!" she cried
and into the neighbouring burrow she dived.

"Good gracious!" she warbled, "The worst one I've seen! That burrow is fit for a pig, not a Queen!"

"I was up to my ankles in **muck** on the floor
and my shiny, gold slippers are **ruined**, I'm sure!

Plus, down in the **dirt**, with the **worms** and the **ants**,

sat a **rat**, wearing only his **underpants!**

Hello there!
You are just in
time for tea!

"The fanciest burrow?
Not likely," she bawled.

"Such **squalor**, such standards,
I'm shocked and appalled!"

But as she was leaving,
she heard them all say,
"Our plan worked a treat,
she is going, hurray!

She may be a rich Queen
with feasts every day,
but caring or thoughtful?
Not likely, no way!"

The Queen felt ashamed and she turned back around.
She looked at the bunnies then looked at the ground.
"You've taught me a lesson," she said, "and I'm glad,
for though I am rich I am lonely and sad."

"I must behave better, I must make amends,
and if you will have me, I'd like to be friends."

"You can come to a ball back at my place," she said,
"and stay overnight in my four poster bed!"
The bunnies looked thrilled. "Will there be a big feast?"
Queen Fluff smiled and nodded, "Ten-courses, at least!"

The End

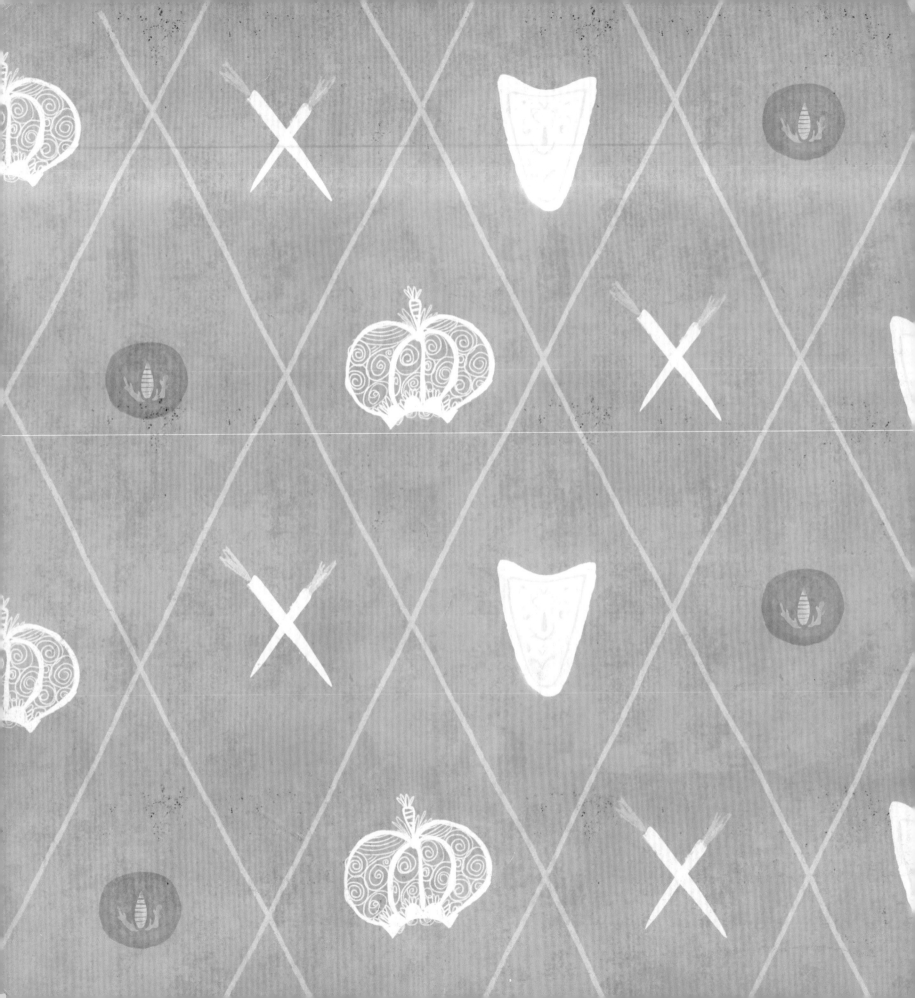

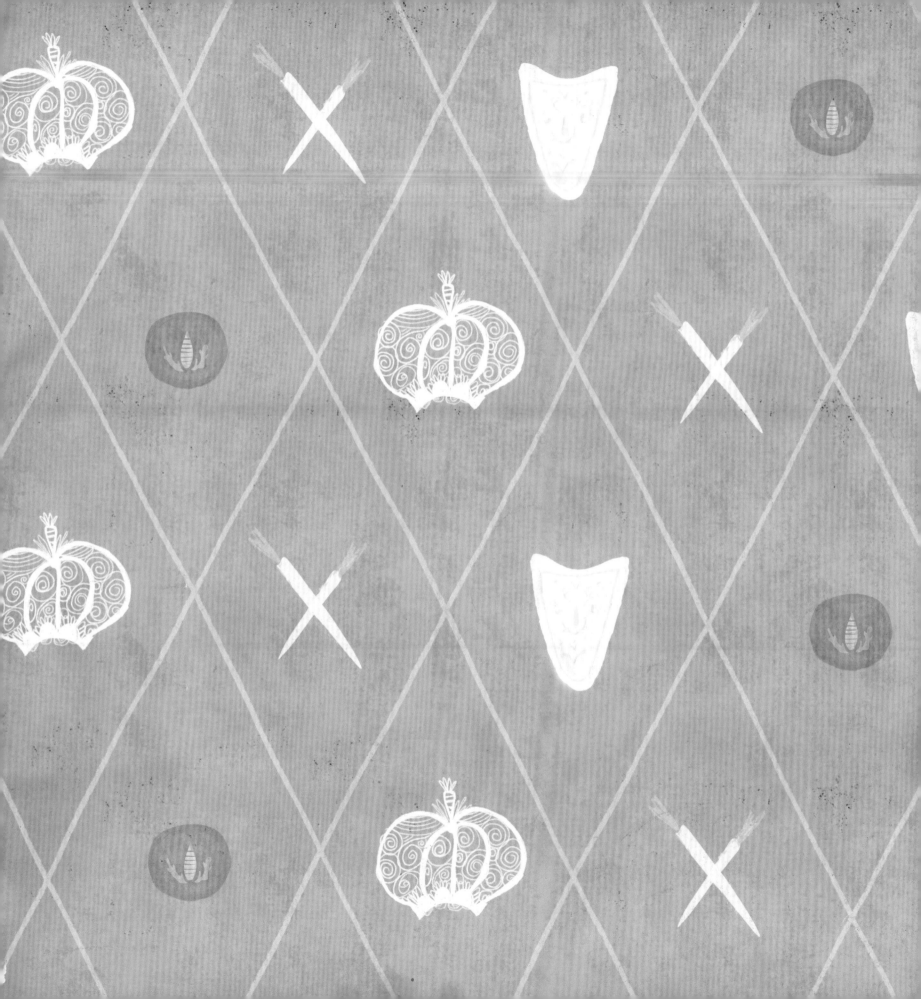

Not Enough for Queen Fluff
is an original concept by © Rachel Lyon

Author: Rachel Lyon

Illustrator: Catalina Echeverri

Published by **MAVERICK ARTS PUBLISHING LTD**
Studio 3A, City Business Centre, 6 Brighton Road,
Horsham, West Sussex, RH13 5BB
© Maverick Arts Publishing Limited May 2016
+44 (0)1403 256941 www.maverickbooks.co.uk

A CIP catalogue record for this book is available
at the British Library.

ISBN 978-1-84886-203-6